Dear Parents:

Congratulations! Your child is taking the first steps on an exciting journey. The destination? Independent reading!

STEP INTO READING® will help your child get there. The program offers five steps to reading success. Each step includes fun stories and colorful art or photographs. In addition to original fiction and books with favorite characters, there are Step into Reading Non-Fiction Readers, Phonics Readers and Boxed Sets, Sticker Readers, and Comic Readers—a complete literacy program with something to interest every child.

Learning to Read, Step by Step!

Ready to Read   Preschool–Kindergarten
• big type and easy words • rhyme and rhythm • picture clues
For children who know the alphabet and are eager to begin reading.

Reading with Help   Preschool–Grade 1
• basic vocabulary • short sentences • simple stories
For children who recognize familiar words and sound out new words with help.

Reading on Your Own   Grades 1–3
• engaging characters • easy-to-follow plots • popular topics
For children who are ready to read on their own.

Reading Paragraphs   Grades 2–3
• challenging vocabulary • short paragraphs • exciting stories
For newly independent readers who read simple sentences with confidence.

Ready for Chapters   Grades 2–4
• chapters • longer paragraphs • full-color art
For children who want to take the plunge into chapter books but still like colorful pictures.

STEP INTO READING® is designed to give every child a successful reading experience. The grade levels are only guides; children will progress through the steps at their own speed, developing confidence in their reading.

Remember, a lifetime love of reading starts with a single step!

Visit us on the Web!
StepIntoReading.com
rhcbooks.com

Educators and librarians, for a variety of teaching tools, visit us at RHTeachersLibrarians.com

ISBN 978-0-525-64865-9 (trade) — ISBN 978-0-525-64866-6 (lib. bdg.)

Printed in the United States of America

10 9 8 7 6 5 4 3 2 1

Ninja Blaze

and his new friends

flip, kick, and spin.

They smash things.

Ninja <u>chop</u>!

Crusher and Pickle
see Ninja Blaze.
They want to be
ninjas, too!

Crusher and Pickle
fly through the air.

Whoops!

Crusher and Pickle

land on a cliff!

They are stuck.

They need help!

AJ and Ninja Blaze can help!
They race to the rescue.

VROOM!

Ninja Blaze and AJ

see a gate,

but it is closed.

Blaze uses
a ninja chop
to break through!

Ninja Blaze and AJ
reach the mountain.
But how will they
get to their friends?

They use a rope and a hook
to climb the mountain.

Oh, no!
Crusher and Pickle
fall off the cliff!
They get stuck
in a snowball!

Ninja Blaze uses
Blazing Speed
to catch up
to his friends.

Then he uses
a ninja chop
to blast the snowball.

Yay!
Crusher and Pickle
are safe.
Time for a ninja party!

Blaze and AJ
meet some ninjas.
They want to be
ninjas, too!

2

STEP

READING WITH HELP

STEP INTO READING®

nickelodeon

NINJA BLAZE!

by C. Ines Mangual

based on the teleplay "Ninja Blaze!"
by Halcyon Person

illustrated by Dave Aikins

Random House 🏠 New York